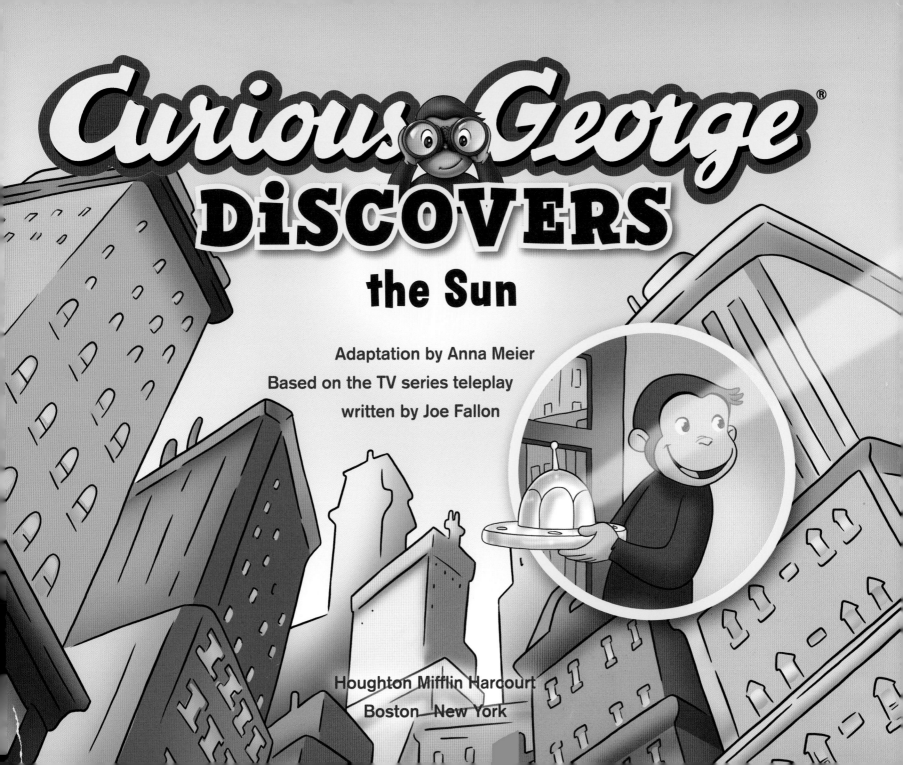

Curious George DISCOVERS

the Sun

Adaptation by Anna Meier

Based on the TV series teleplay

written by Joe Fallon

Houghton Mifflin Harcourt

Boston   New York

Top photograph on front cover and photographs on pp. 3, 9, 15, 22, 25, 31 courtesy of HMH/Carrie Garcia

Bottom photograph on front cover courtesy of NASA

Photographs on pp. 7, 12 courtesy of HMH/Guy Jarvis

Photographs on p. 18 courtesy of HMH/Steve Williams

Top photograph on p. 21 courtesy of NASA/SDO/AIA/GSFC

Other images courtesy of HMH

For information about permission to reproduce selections from this book, write to Permissions, Houghton Mifflin Harcourt Publishing Company, 215 Park Avenue South, New York, New York 10003.

ISBN: 978-0-544-45426-2 paper over board
ISBN: 978-0-544-43067-9 paperback

Design by Susanna Vagt
www.hmhco.com
Printed in China
SCP 10 9 8 7 6 5 4 3 2 1
4500515589

George was a good
very curious. Even
the hottest day o
George learned a
not, our story sta

George loved playing outside on warm days, but today he needed a break from the sun. "Too hot for the park, George?" asked the man with the yellow hat. George nodded and went over to the air conditioner. Just as George started enjoying the cool air, the air conditioner turned off! So did everything else: the lights, the fan, the radio. This was a sign of very hot weather—a blackout.

"I should call the electric company so they know we have no power," the man said. The cordless phone wasn't in its battery charger, though. Where could it be?

George found the phone on top of the air conditioner, but it was no use! Since it hadn't been charging, there was no more power left in its batteries.

"We're due at the museum, George. We can call from there," the man said.

When they got to the museum, it was dark there, too. "Still no electricity?" the man with the yellow hat asked Professor Wiseman.

"There is for us!" she said, as she flipped the light switch and all the lights flickered on. How could the museum have power when the rest of the city didn't? George wondered if the blackout was over. "Let's go up to the roof. I have something to show you," said Professor Wiseman.

Professor Wiseman's friend Dr. Levitt was waiting for them on the roof of the museum. "You just witnessed the first test of the solar panels I installed to power the museum!" Dr. Levitt said.

"We're unveiling them at a party tonight," said Professor Wiseman. "We're a solar museum! Do you know what *solar-powered* means, George?" He didn't.

Professor Wiseman explained, "Usually electricity is made far away and sent in on wires, but now the museum can make its own power."

"Solar panels turn the sun's rays into electricity," said Dr. Levitt, "which is then stored in batteries."

Did you know . . .

that solar energy is better for our environment? The sun is a source of energy that is renewable. That means we won't run out of it. Solar power also doesn't pollute the air. This makes it a source of energy we can continue using forever without hurting the environment.

Dr. Levitt showed the big blue batteries to George. "These batteries are a lot like the ones in toys, flashlights, or cordless phones. And they get all their power from the sun!"

George never knew the sun could charge batteries—did you?

"It's Dr. Levitt's birthday," Professor Wiseman whispered to the man with the yellow hat. "During the party for the solar panels, I'd like to give her a surprise."

"I could make my famous veggie lasagna," the man whispered back.

"Precisely what I was thinking!" Professor Wiseman agreed.

Back at home, the electricity had turned back on. The man was going to get started on his lasagna, so George picked out his remote control spaceship to play with. It was the perfect indoor toy for a hot day.

That is, until the batteries ran out.

Did you know . . .
without batteries things such as flashlights, phones, and remote control toys would have to be plugged into an electrical outlet to work? Batteries store energy. When the energy runs out, they have to be recharged or replaced.

George didn't want to bother the man while he was making lasagna, but he needed batteries. Then George remembered how the museum batteries got power from the sun! So what do you think he did?

He put his spaceship out in the sun. Then he thought there might be some other things that needed charging. So he grabbed the phone, a flashlight, and a couple of batteries, and set them out in the sun to charge too!

Inside, the man was assembling his lasagna: noodles, vegetables, sauce, and cheese. It would be a perfect birthday surprise!

"Professor Wiseman didn't say what time to bring this," he said. "I'd better call her. George, have you seen the phone?"

George showed him the objects on the table outside in the sun. When the man tried to use the phone, though, it still wasn't charged. George was confused. He reached for the batteries that had been sitting in the sun. Ouch! They were very hot!

"That's not how solar power works, George. The sun can't charge the batteries like this, but it can make things hot—especially when it reflects off something shiny."

Since the phone still didn't work, George took a note from the man to Professor Wiseman at the museum. When he got there, he was very hot. "Back again, George?" she asked. "In this heat?"

She read the note and told George, "Ask him to bring his lasagna over at six o'clock." As she wrote down the time on the note, George noticed something different about Professor Wiseman's car.

"Those are solar panels, George! They convert the sun's rays to electric power, remember?" she said. Of course! George had forgotten about solar panels when he set the phone out in the sun. Now he remembered: the sun shines on the solar panels, the panels turn the sun's rays into energy, and the batteries store that energy.

"Hey, want a ride home in a solar car?" Boy, did he! It would sure beat walking in the heat.

When George and Professor Wiseman pulled up to George's building, they startled Hundley and the doorman.

"I didn't even hear that car drive up!" exclaimed the doorman.

"That's because solar-powered engines are quiet. See you tonight, George!" called Professor Wiseman as she drove away.

Did you know . . .

the first electric car was built more than a hundred years ago? Different models of electric cars have been created ever since. Electric motors are much quieter than gas engines and are better for the environment. Gasoline, which fuels most cars, pollutes the air. This is why it's good to walk or ride a bike whenever you can, and to carpool when you need to drive in a car. Some cars are called hybrids and can be powered by both gas and electricity.

George gave the note to the man with the yellow hat.

"Six o'clock," he said. "If I put it in the oven right now, it'll be ready in plenty of time."

The man put the lasagna in the oven and turned on the heat.

But a minute later, the oven shut off again. So did the fan, the radio, and the lights! "Another blackout!" said the man. "George, the oven is electric. My lasagna won't cook. I'd better warn Professor Wiseman that we may be late, or worse—lasagna-less!" he said.

But the phone was still dead. He'd forgotten to put it back on the battery charger again.

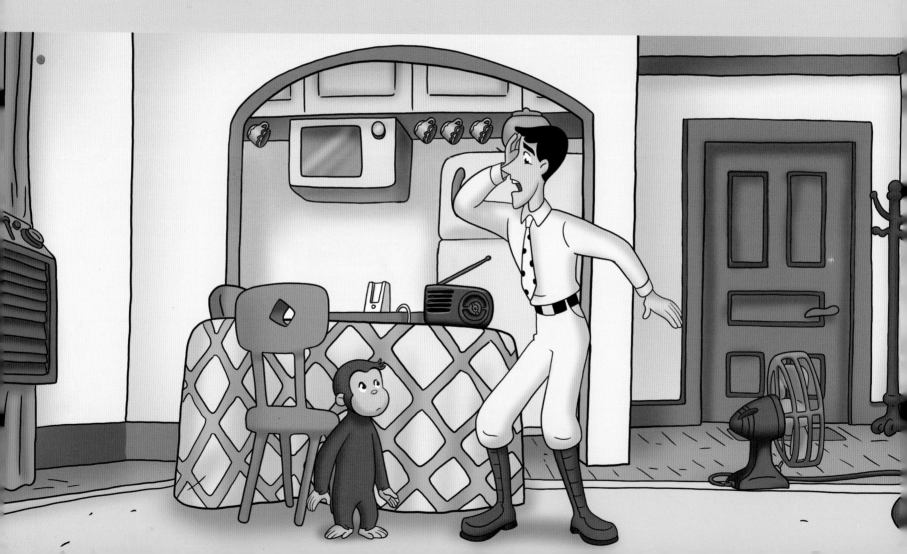

"There's no way to cook without power," the man said as he set the uncharged phone down again.

Or was there?

George noticed the sun reflecting off his toy spaceship and remembered something his friend had said earlier: the sun can make things very hot if it's reflected off a shiny surface.

Earth to Scale

Did you know . . .

the sun is really a giant star? The sun is 100 times bigger than Earth, and it is so bright because it's the closest star to Earth. The heat from the sun travels millions of miles to reach us, but those other tiny stars that you see at night are light-years away—and that's really far! What's the farthest you've ever traveled?

That gave George an idea! He pointed his spaceship so the sun reflected off of it into the man's eyes. "George, that reflected sun is bright," he said, "and hot."

But then he realized what George was trying to tell him. They could use the heat of the sun to cook the lasagna!

"George, you may be a genius!" the man exclaimed.

They found a pizza box from one of the last week's dinners at Chef Pisghetti's restaurant.

"A pizza box keeps pizza warm, so it will trap the heat," the man said as he began to cut a flap into the top of the box. "We'll need a hole to let the sun in."

The man continued to give instructions to build their solar-powered oven. "Glue on some plastic wrap to keep the heat from getting out," he said.

"And shiny aluminum foil to direct the sun's heat into the box."

Once that was done, they placed the lasagna inside the pizza box and brought it outside.

"Angle the top so that the sun hits the lasagna, George," the man said. "If the power comes back on, we can put it in the oven. But if it doesn't, I think this will cook."

At six o'clock that evening, guests arrived at the museum.
It was the only building in the whole city with electricity!

George and the man with the yellow hat arrived—with the special birthday lasagna!

Professor Wiseman gasped as they opened the pizza box. "It's hot!" she exclaimed. "Thank goodness the surprise isn't ruined!"

Inside, all the guests sat at a long table to celebrate both the museum's solar power and Dr. Levitt's birthday.

Now the lasagna would be even more of a surprise since the whole city had been without power for cooking!

"Oh my!" Dr. Levitt said when she saw the steaming lasagna. "How did you cook it during the blackout?"

"We made a solar cooker," the man said. "Thank George . . . and the sun."

Dr. Levitt was thrilled. It was a wonderful surprise. "Nothing could make this birthday more special than a solar lasagna!"

Meltdown Experiment

The light from the sun reflects differently off light colors than it does off dark colors. Dark objects take in sunlight, and therefore get hotter faster. Light objects reflect sunlight. Since light bounces off them, they get hot less quickly. To test this theory, let's do an experiment!

You will need . . .

- 1 black sheet of paper
- 1 white sheet of paper
- 2 ice cubes of similar size
- a sunny day

Directions:

Take both pieces of paper outside on a sunny day and set them on the ground or another flat surface next to each other. Make sure you're not in a shaded area and that the sun is shining directly onto your pieces of paper equally. Then place an ice cube on each sheet of paper and watch to see which one melts fastest. Can you guess which one will melt first?

Explore further:

You can also try this experiment using a variety of colors! Try melting ice cubes at the same time on a yellow, blue, or red sheet of paper. Can you guess which colors will cause the ice cube to melt the fastest? Which will cause the ice cube to melt the slowest?

Build your own solar oven!

George and his friend couldn't use their oven when the power went out, so they built an oven that would cook their food with the sun's heat. You can do the same thing to make a delicious snack on a hot summer day!

You will need . . .

- 1 box with a lid (a pizza box or a shoebox works well)
- aluminum foil
- scissors
- tape or glue
- black construction paper
- plastic wrap
- a craft stick
- the ingredients for your snack (try cooking a mini pizza made out of an English muffin with sauce and shredded cheese, or s'mores with graham crackers, marshmallows, and chocolate!)

Directions:

Take the lid off your box and ask an adult to cut three sides of a rectangle in the center of your box's lid to create a flap. Tape or glue a piece of foil to the inside of the flap.

Line the inside of your box with aluminum foil with the shinier side facing down. Tape or glue the foil in place. Now, put your black piece of paper in the bottom of the box.

Next, stretch the plastic wrap very tightly over the opening in the lid and tape or glue it into place.

Assemble the ingredients for your snack, place it inside the box, and put the lid on. Prop the flap open with the craft stick and some tape. Set your solar oven outside in a spot where it's sure to get lots of sunlight. Check back every fifteen minutes or so until your snack is ready to eat!

Make a sundial!

You don't need a watch or a clock to tell the time. Learn to tell what time it is using the shadows created by the sun!

You will need . . .

- sunshine
- 1 paper plate
- 1 plastic straw
- tape
- crayons or markers
- sharpened pencil
- small rocks

Directions:

1. Use your crayons or markers to write the numbers 1 to 12 on your paper plate, just like on the face of a clock. Ask an adult to help you make sure that all the numbers are spaced evenly.

2. If you like, you can also decorate your plate with drawings.

3. Use the pencil to poke a hole through the exact center of the plate.

4. Place the straw in the hole and secure it on the other side of the plate with tape.

Using your sundial:

At noon, take your plate outside and set it on a flat surface in plenty of sunshine. Slowly turn your plate until the straw's shadow falls on the number 12. Place a few small rocks on your plate to keep it from moving. Now you can use your sundial to tell the time whenever the sun is shining! As time goes by, simply look at where the straw's shadow is falling to know what time it is.

Explore further:

Throughout the day, it looks as if the sun is moving across the sky since it rises in the east and sets in the west. However, the sun actually stays in one place as the earth moves around the sun and rotates at the same time. Because it takes twenty-four hours for Earth to make a complete rotation around the sun, that is the length of a single day.